a bedtime story
written by Anna Richardson
illustrated by Meggie Hunley

Printed in China - First Printing, 2014

ISBN 978-0-615-78640-7

purple
pancakes

Cincinnati, OH 45233
purple-pancakes.com

Dedicated to my chili beans:
Frick, Frack, Fergie and Farfanoogen...
I love you more than my luggage!
-A

Dedicated to my little peanut
...and any future mix of nuts.
-M

Luke is a good boy
He's four years old
He's kind to his siblings
And does what he's told

That is until dark
When bedtime rolls around
He hops on Daddy's back
And lets out a loud sound...
Aaaaaggghhhhh!

Lay with me Daddy
Don't leave me in bed
There are two green hippos
And a third one that's red

They come in my room
The minute you leave
The green ones just argue
The red one's named Steve

If they don't show up
Then the pink monster will
He wears a tiara and tutu
But says his name's Bill

Bill can be funny
But the outfit's just weird
He's got stinky toots
And he has a green beard

And if it's not Bill
Then Fran will appear
She's a giant red alligator
That wears scuba gear

She stares at my baseball cards
And says they look yummy
I know that she'll steal them
To stuff in her tummy

Please Daddy, please
I'm scared when you go
Just sleep with me here
It means more than you know

Hey little buddy
Calm down and you'll see
I got you this gift
And he got down on his knee

It's a brave superhero
He stays here with you
He protects you from monsters
And gives you strength too

He keeps close watch all night
So that children can dream
You're brave and he's tough
Together you're a team

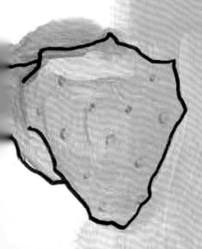

He has special powers
And this cool changing light
To help you stay here in bed
All through the night

The red light on his chest
Means you're brave like him too
You stay here in bed
And here's what he'll do

When it's the right time
To wake up in the morning
The light will turn green
And without any warning

This means you can get up
And find Mom and Dad
To tell them you made it
And you're no longer sad

You're a big boy for sure
You overcame your fears
With the help of your buddy
There's no need now for tears

Now it's up to you, little one
No need to be ashamed
You have a friend to help you
Let's give him his very own name